DAREDEVIL DAYS

Adapted by Molly McGuire

Based on the series created by Dan Povenmire & Jeff "Swampy" Marsh

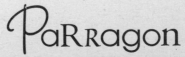

Bath · New York · Singapore · Hong Kong · Cologne · Delhi
Melbourne · Amsterdam · Johannesburg · Auckland · Shenzhen

This edition published by Parragon in 2011

Parragon
Queen Street House
4 Queen Street
Bath BA1 1HE, UK

ISBN 978-1-4454-5018-6
Printed and bound by CPI Group (UK) Ltd, Croydon, CR0 4YY

Part One

Chapter 1

It was another glorious day of the summer holidays. Phineas Flynn and Ferb Fletcher were sitting down on the living room sofa with Phineas's grandparents, Grandma Betty Jo and Grandpa Clyde. They were all listening to Mr Fletcher giving an exciting speech on antique thimbles.

"And that is why the eighteenth-century sewing thimble is not only a slice of history,

but a compelling example of American grit and perseverance . . ." Mr Fletcher said, reading from his note card. He would be speaking in front of a large crowd that afternoon and wanted to practise his speech one last time. He looked at his family eagerly.

"Great, Dad!" Phineas said. Mr Fletcher knew everything there was to know about antiques - which was a good thing, because he owned an antique store in town.

"Oh, that was wonderful!" Grandma Betty Jo cheered. Then she dropped her head and pretended to snore loudly.

"Mum!", scolded Mrs Flynn, Phineas's mother.

"Oh, I'm kidding!" Grandma Betty Jo said with a chuckle. She smiled at Mr Fletcher. "Your speech is going to be a big hit at the antique-thimble conference."

Phineas's mum looked down at her watch. "Which we're going to be late for if we don't get on the road," she reminded him. "Thanks again for looking after the kids today," she said to her parents. "Candace is skating at the park. All the numbers are on the fridge."

"Please be good for your grandparents, boys!" Mr Fletcher called to the boys as he and his wife left the house.

Phineas and Ferb waved goodbye. The house seemed strangely quiet. What were they going to do all day? Even Perry, the boys' pet platypus, looked a little bored.

But then their grandmother gave them a sly smile. "You want to go down and embarrass

your sister at the park?" she asked.

"Yeah! Yeah!" Phineas and Grandpa Clyde cheered in unison.

The boys and their grandparents dashed

out of the room, leaving Perry staring blankly after them. The day was getting better already!

* * *

At the park, Candace's best friend, Stacy Hirano, was helping Candace roller-skate. "You got it!" Stacy cheered, skating in front of Candace. "You may be rusty, but you got it!"

Stacy was a natural skater. Candace Flynn, on the other hand . . . was not. She was a whiz when it came to shopping and singing and acting - but skating wasn't her thing.

"I - I can't turn around or stop, but I got it!" Candace was flailing her arms, frantically trying to keep her balance. "I wonder if Jeremy's skating here today," she said. Jeremy

Johnson was a classmate of Candace and Stacy and he worked at the local burger joint. Candace had a megacrush on him. In Candace's eyes, Jeremy was absolutely the cutest guy on the entire planet.

Suddenly, Stacy stopped skating, causing Candace to nearly crash into her. Stacy pointed across the park. "Isn't that your family?" she asked. Candace's mouth dropped open. What were they doing there?! She spotted Ferb roller-skating nearby in graceful circles.

"See, I told you Ferb was a good skater," Phineas said to his grandma, beaming proudly. They were all decked out in their skating helmets and elbow and knee pads. Grandpa Clyde was sitting on a nearby bench, watching all the action.

"Ooh, that's my boy!" Grandma Betty Jo cooed, admiring Ferb's technique. She and Phineas joined Ferb out on the pavement and

skated dazzling loops and spins around one another. A crowd had gathered to watch them. They were really good!

Suddenly, Grandpa Clyde spotted Candace skating down the path. "Yoo-hoo!" he called to her. "Hello!" Grandma Betty Jo shouted, waving wildly at Candace.

"Hey, Candace, jump in!" Phineas yelled as he spun around in a circle.

Suddenly, Candace stopped short and

looked over at her brothers and grandparents in horror. "Turn me around, Stacy!"
she commanded. Stacy pointed her friend in
the opposite direction and they rolled away
from Candace's family. Candace was not
happy. Leave it to Phineas to spoil a perfectly
pleasant day at the park! I'll get you, Phineas!
she thought.

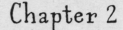

Chapter 2

Grandma Betty Jo, Phineas and Ferb skated through the park on a sunlit path.

"So Grandma, where did you get your moves?" Phineas asked her. He'd never seen another grandma who could roller-skate even half as well as his could!

Phineas's grandmother glided out in front of them and gracefully jumped in the air. "You see, boys, I really was quite the skater in my - OOOF!" She hadn't been watching where she was going and she'd run right into someone! She fell to the ground with a grunt. "Watch where you're - " she had started to say. Then she stopped in midsentence. The other skater looked vaguely familiar to her.

That other skater had the same thought. "Betty Jo of the Tri-

State Bombers?" she asked. She looked about the same age as Grandma Betty Jo and she had short, white hair.

"Hildegard? Of the Saskatoon Slashers?" Betty Jo asked, totally surprised. She took off her eyeglasses to get a closer look at the woman she'd crashed into.

Hildegard put her hands on her hips. "I thought I'd smelled the last of you back in 1957, when I took the trophy and became the rightful queen of the derby," she said with a sneer.

"Whoa! Grandma, you were in a roller-skating derby?" Phineas asked in surprise.

"Not only was I in it, I was champ! It was years ago." His grandma got a faraway look in her eye as she recalled the final roller-derby match between the Tri-State Bombers and the Saskatoon Slashers.

"We were in our final lap. My team used our signature move, the Whip, to send me over the

13

finish line." She explained that the Whip was a difficult move skaters used when heading around a curve. They formed a human chain and the person on the outside of the chain would fly forward with a burst of speed when they whipped around the bend. It sounded pretty tricky . . . and also pretty dangerous. My grandma's a speed demon, Phineas thought. Cool!

"Hildegard's skating team had exacty the

same idea," Grandma Betty Jo continued. Then she described how both she and Hildegard had approached the finish line at exactly the same time. Just when she was about to cross it, Hildegard reached out . . . and shoved her! Phineas and Ferb gasped. That didn't sound fair at all!

"You only won because you cheated!" Grandma Betty Jo exclaimed, turning to face her old rival.

"'Anything goes,' remember?" Hildegard replied, repeating an old roller-derby saying. She narrowed her eyes.

Grandma Betty Jo and Hildegard squared off like cowboys about to draw for a duel. "Well, what do you say we try it again?" Grandma Betty Jo challenged.

"Anytime, anywhere!" Hildegard replied.

"You skate like a water buffalo!" Grandma Betty Jo spat.

"You couldn't win a race against a one-

15

legged, stuffed owl!" Hildegard yelled.

Phineas smelled a rematch! He couldn't wait to see his grandma in action.

* * *

A few moments later, Candace skated over to them, her eyes wide with shock at the sight of her grandma and another lady yelling at each other. Just then, Jeremy skidded to a stop right behind Candace. He'd been skating on his own in a different area of the park.

"Hi, Jeremy," Candace said, gazing at him dreamily. How romantic to practically be skating together, she thought. Or at least standing next to each other while wearing skates. It was progress!

"Uh, Candace, why is my grandma yelling at your grandma?" Jeremy asked, frowning.

Candace suddenly snapped out of the daydream she'd been having where she and Jeremy skated off into the sunset together, holding hands. "That's your grandmother?!" she

cried, pointing in surprise at the threatening-looking woman who was now barreling toward them.

"Come on then please Jeremy! You and your little sister can be on my team!" Hildegard shouted. "Suzy!" she hollered. Jeremy dutifully followed his grandmother as a cute little girl with bright blue eyes and blond ringlets skated down the hill.

"Yes, Grandma?" Suzy asked innocently, her eyes wide.

"Me, you and Jeremy are a team, got it?" Hildegard said gruffly.

Suzy smiled sweetly and fluttered her eyelashes. She was ready for this challenge!

Meanwhile, Grandma

Betty Jo was rounding up her own team for the rematch. "So I need two of you kids on my team, okay?" she said.

"Well," Candace began slowly. No way was she getting roped into this one - especially with Jeremy on the other team! "You can have Phineas and Ferb, Grandma, I'm not - "

"But that's not fair, Candace," Suzy interrupted in her sweetest voice. "Our team has two girls and one boy, so you need to be on your grandma's team so it's fair. Because it's not fair if it's two boys and one girl against

two girls and one boy!" Suzy flashed her most innocent-looking smile.

Candace narrowed her eyes at Jeremy's little sister. She knew that this was all an act. Suzy was very protective of Jeremy and wanted to keep Candace far away from him.

Phineas pointed at his sister. "Then it's you, Ferb and Grandma! You'll make a great team!" he cheered.

"But -" Candace protested. Skating wasn't her thing! How was Jeremy supposed to realize how fabulous she was when she could barely stand up in a pair of skates?

"Well, I guess it's set then. We have to do it for our grandmas. Right, Candace?" Jeremy said with a smile.

"Yeah, right . . ." Candace said, staring at Jeremy. She chuckled nervously. "Right." Then she felt someone tap

her sharply on the back. She spun around and looked down to see Jeremy's sister grinning evilly at her.

"Psst!" Suzy hissed quietly. "See you on the track, chump!" And with that, she raced away, doing a complicated twirl just to show Candace who was boss.

"Yeah, great," Candace said with a sigh. But then she thought of something. "Hey! Wait!" she said excitedly to the rest of the group. "There's nowhere to have a roller-skating derby, remember? The old derby track got torn down and turned into a tattoo parlour!" Victory! Candace thought. She wouldn't have to skate after all!

"Leave the rink to us," Phineas said slyly. He and Ferb would come up with a plan. They always did!

Candace slumped her shoulders. "How am I going to get out of this one?" she thought. "This is so not good!"

Chapter 3

Meanwhile, Perry the Platypus, aka Agent P, wasn't just sitting around at home doing nothing. He had packed himself into a large parcel, with the correct postage, to be delivered to his top secret headquarters under Phineas and Ferb's house. You see, Perry wasn't just an ordinary family pet. He was also a top secret agent in charge of making sure the evil Dr Doofenshmirtz never achieved domination

of the tri-state area. It was a time-consuming job, but somebody had to do it.

Perry dropped through the mail chute onto his desk chair, popped out of the box and looked around the high-tech Platypus Cave. Now he just had to wait for orders from his superior officer, Major Monogram.

Just then, Major Monogram's face appeared above Perry's desk, broadcast via a huge satellite monitor. "Hmm . . . Nice entrance, Agent P," he said. "But you do realize there is a lift over there, right?"

Perry glanced at the lift and then turned back to the screen. He knew perfectly well there was a lift there, but he preferred to travel undercover. He was a top-ranking spy, after all.

"Okay," Major Monogram said. "Back to business. Dr Doofenshmirtz is up to something. I want you to get out there and put a stop to it."

Perry nodded. He knew that the evil doctor had a long history of being up to no good and only Perry could put an end to it. Agent P gave a salute to his boss and got to work.

Moments later, Agent P was sneaking into Doofenshmirtz Evil Incorporated headquarters across town. He climbed a wall of the giant building and balanced carefully on a window ledge to get a peek inside. Dr Doofenshmirtz

was staring out of another window. Perry leaped into the room, landing softly on his webbed feet. He assumed a karate stance and waited quietly for his enemy to turn away from the window on the other side of the room.

"Will you cool it with the noise, Perry the Platypus?" Dr Doofenshmirtz said. "I've got a splitting headache." He turned around and didn't look at all surprised to see Perry. "Can you hang out for just one moment? I'm almost there."

Dr Doofenshmirtz walked a few steps and hit a yellow button that was mounted on the wall. Directly above Perry, a metal cage came crashing down from the ceiling. Before Agent P could react, the cage trapped the platypus inside with a clatter. Dr Doofenshmirtz held his head and sighed. "Ow! I've got to get a

quieter trap!"

Perry shook the bars of the cage, but it was no use. He was locked inside. This was not a desirable situation for a spy to find

himself in!

Dr Doofenshmirtz struggled to carry the cage with Perry inside. The doctor was huffing and puffing as he talked. "Now that you're trapped, I will tell you my evil plan! I'm miserable because I can't grow facial hair. It all started when I was about fifteen . . ." the evil doctor began. "I've tried everything. It's all

so painful."

He finally managed to shove Perry's cage up against a window. He wiped his brow, breathing heavily and pointed outside.

"So, who do they erect a statue of right next door? Rutherford B. Hayes, our nineteenth president! Only the president with the best facial hair of all! Just look at that thing!" Dr Doofenshmirtz stared angrily out of the window.

Perry peered between the bars of his cage into the grassy courtyard below. Standing in the centre of the square was a statue of a man with a very bushy beard and moustache. He was quite hairy indeed!

"There's no beard like a nineteenth-century beard, Perry the Platypus," the doctor

said. "Anyway, that horrible statue must be destroyed, as it's a constant reminder of my follicle failure!" the villain yelled, clenching his fists.

Agent P glared at his enemy. How was he ever going to escape and save the statue from being destroyed?

Candace and Stacy had headed back to Candace's house. Candace couldn't stop worrying about the roller derby.

"I can't be a part of this race!" Candace cried. She just absolutely, one hundred percent, could not skate in the rematch. And it wasn't only because her skating skills weren't top-notch. "I mean, what if we win? Would Jeremy still like me?" she asked nervously.

"All I know for sure is that boys hate to be beaten by girls," Stacy said matter-of-factly.

Candace frowned. What was a girl to do in a situation like this?

Just then, Grandpa Clyde poked his head over the backyard fence. "There you are," he said to Candace. "Do you know where your dad keeps his glue gun?"

"Glue gun? What are they up to?" Candace wondered aloud. "Later Stace - " she said and dashed after her grandfather. Whatever they were doing, Candace felt certain it was something they shouldn't be. She'd catch Phineas this time around!

Candace found Phineas, Ferb and her grandfather huddled together in the backyard. "I knew it!" she exclaimed, looking around. They had built a giant, stadium-size roller-derby rink right on the lawn! Above the entrance they'd hung a big banner that said REMATCH! "I just knew you'd be up to something by now!" Candace yelled. She glared at Phineas. Then she flipped open her mobile phone. "Just wait until Mum hears about this!"

Suddenly, her grandmother skated into

the backyard. "Heads up!" she shouted as she tossed a helmet in Candace's direction. Then she handed Candace a pair of skates. "Lace 'em up tight, dearie. We've got a score to settle. Win! Win! Win!" she chanted. She put a roller-skate in her mouth and shook it from side to side, like a lion wrestling with its prey.

"Yeah!" Phineas cheered. This was going to be one great rematch!

Chapter 4

It was almost time for the roller-derby rematch to begin. Grandma Betty Jo was in the changing room that Phineas, Ferb and Grandpa Clyde had built. She was giving Candace and Ferb a pre-derby pep talk.

"And then on the final lap, we'll use the Whip to launch the weak skater - no offense, honey, but that's you" - she said, pointing at Candace - "over the finish line to victory!" Grandma Betty Jo pumped her fists in the air.

She couldn't wait for the competition to start!

Stacy's words echoed in Candace's head: All I know for sure is that boys hate to be beaten by girls. . . . Candace was super nervous. What if they won? She could see it now: Candace holding up the roller-derby trophy, the crowd going wild . . . Jeremy consoling his grandmother. He would never talk to Candace again. This was going to be a disaster!

"And remember, honey," Grandma Betty Jo said, skating out of the locker room, "show 'em no mercy!"

"What am I going to do?" Candace groaned

as she sat alone on a changing room bench. "I can't beat Jeremy's grandmother and I can't let my grandmother lose." It was a totally impossible situation!

As Candace sat there worrying, Suzy snuck into the changing room. Candace was so deep in thought that she didn't even see her. With a sinister grin, Suzy quickly swapped Candace's skates for another pair and then hurried out of the room. Candace reached for her skates just as an announcer came over the loudspeaker: "Skaters to their marks!"

"Oh, that's great," Candace muttered. She slowly put on her skates. "Maybe I'll get lucky and get hit by a bus."

Outside the changing room, Phineas had assumed the role of announcer. High above the rink in the press box, he addressed the crowd.

"Hello, everyone!" he began. "Welcome to today's main event: the 'Anything Goes' roller-skate grudge race of the century between Grandma Betty Jo and Grandma Hildegard. I'm Phineas Flynn and I'll be your announcer for today's action, along with our colour commentator, Grandpa Clyde." Phineas leaned over and held the microphone toward his grandfather.

"Yellow! Green! Blue!" Grandpa Clyde shouted into the mic.

"Excellent colour, Grandpa," Phineas said approvingly.

"Glad to oblige," Grandpa Clyde said to Phineas, smiling.

"And now . . ." Phineas's voice boomed out

over the speakers. "Let's rock and roller-skate derby!"

The crowd went wild. Phineas grinned to himself. It was showtime!

On the rink, all the skaters were lined up at the starting line - well, almost all the skaters. Candace came to a shaky stop next to her teammates before she fell down. OOF! She looked up unhappily from the ground. She would have chosen a shopping trip over this any day!

Hildegard and her team assumed their own starting positions. She leaned in closer to Jeremy and Suzy. "Remember, kids," she said

with a serious look on her face. "One word: roadkill."

"Come on, honey!" Grandma Betty Jo said to Candace, who was

still lying facedown on the floor of the rink. "We've got butt to kick!"

Up in the press box, Grandpa Clyde pulled the trigger on a starter pistol. And the race began!

Candace struggled to her feet just in time and the skaters started speeding around the track.

"And they're off!" Phineas shouted.

Grandma Betty Jo and Hildegard accelerated, leaning forward into the wind. Ferb settled into an easy skating stride and kept pace with Suzy, who was trying her best to trip him. Candace and Jeremy were toward the back. The dueling  grannies quickly left their teammates in the dust, as if they were the only two skaters on the rink. This was definitely a grudge match!

Chapter 5

The roller-derby competition was fierce! "We're coming to the end of the race. The crowd is going nuts!" Phineas's voice bellowed from the loudspeaker.

But Candace was running out of steam. That is, until her grandmother skated up behind her and grabbed her hand. "Come on, Candace! Time for the Whip!" She was getting ready to break out her old team's signature move.

Grandma Betty Jo held Ferb's hand on one side and Candace's on the other. They accelerated on their way into the final curve, preparing to launch Candace out in front. But Hildegard wasn't going down without a fight! She and her team were barrelling towards the very same curve in their own crack-the-whip formation! Who was going to pull off the move first? Candace flew around the corner and came out of the Whip with a burst of speed. She was in first place!

"Go catch her, Jeremy!" cried Suzy.

"It's Candace and Jeremy neck and neck as they come down the straight!" Phineas yelled. Candace looked over and saw that Jeremy was skating just as fast as she was. Uh-oh, Candace thought. What if I beat him?

But little did they know that Suzy was

right behind them and she was about to take matters into her own hands.

"I don't think so," she muttered as she pulled out a remote control. She flipped a single red switch to activate the skates Candace was wearing - the very same ones Suzy herself had swapped for Candace's normal skates in the changing room! Suddenly, two rocket engines shot out of the sides of Candace's skates. ZOOM! With a fiery blast, Candace was hurled backwards. She catapulted towards the stands and the power of her jet-engine skates flung her into the crowd.

Candace tried not to panic. She picked herself up, raced backwards up the stadium steps, ricocheted off the top row of seats and spun through the air. The crowd anxiously held its breath. A few seconds later, Candace landed -

amazingly - right back on the rink, just a couple of paces behind Jeremy!

"But wait! Candace and Jeremy are back in the race . . . but they're going the wrong way!" Phineas cried.

It was true - Candace had made it back to the rink. Only now she was headed in the wrong direction - and she was totally out of control!

Candace and Jeremy slammed into Suzy at full speed and then into Ferb. Now they were all speeding in the opposite direction to the finish line - and right towards their grandmas! Just as the kids braced themselves for a giant collision, both grandmothers leaped over them, sailing through the air.

Grandma Betty Jo came down first and then

Hildegard landed right on Grandma Betty Jo's shoulders. Hildegard was covering her rival's eyes as she tried to hang on.

"Get off me! I can't see!" Grandma Betty Jo shouted as the two grannies wrestled, barrelling toward the finish line.

"It's Grandma Betty! It's Hildegard! It's Betty! It's Hildegard!" Phineas announced, struggling to keep up with the play-by-play. This was the closest roller-derby race he'd ever seen!

Just then, the dueling grandmas crossed the finish line in a blur. The crowd was silent. It wasn't clear who had won the race!

But Phineas had been paying close attention. "It's a tie!" he shouted. The crowd went wild.

Grandpa Clyde awoke from a small catnap he'd been taking just in time to hear Phineas's announcement. "Oh, Betty Jo isn't going to like that," he warned.

Back on the rink, the grannies still had a score to settle. "Well, at least I won this race!" Grandma Betty Jo proclaimed.

"You won?! You're crazy," Hildegard replied.

41

She was still sitting on Grandma Betty Jo's shoulders. "I obviously crossed the finish line first."

"Wrong! And, get off!" Grandma Betty Jo shrugged her shoulders and Hildegard crashed to the ground with a loud thud!

Candace skated excitedly toward her grandmother. "Hey, Grandma, that was really fun!" she exclaimed. "I thought it would be totally lame and I'd hate it, but I had fun!" She gave her grandmother a big hug.

Grandma Betty Jo turned towards her old rival, who was sitting on the ground with Jeremy and Suzy. "What about you, Hilda? Did you have fun?" she asked, giving her a small smile.

"Yeah, I did," Hildegard admitted. "Maybe it's not so important who won, as long as we had fun with the kids."

Grandma Betty Jo agreed. "Yeah, maybe it's not so important." She paused. "But just for the record, I won!"

As the grandkids looked on anxiously, the two ladies squared off again.

"You mean, even though you lost, it's having fun that's important!" Hildegard shouted.

Grandma Betty Jo narrowed her eyes at Hildegard. "Race you to the Rutherford B. Hayes statue!" she challenged. "Go!" The grannies sped off once more on their skates, leaving their grandkids behind.

Here we go again! Phineas thought.

Back at Evil Incorporated H.Q. Perry was still

trapped in his cage. Dr Doofenshmirtz pushed the trap away from the window. "So, Perry the Platypus, in order to rid myself of that horrid bearded statue, I've invented the . . ." The evil doctor stopped in mid-sentence and grunted, exhausted from trying to push Perry's cage. "Ugh! Perry the Platypus, this is so heavy. Can you just step out for a second?" he complained. He unlocked the door of Perry's metal trapand the platypus stepped out. Well, that was easy, Perry thought.

Dr Doofenshmirtz led Agent P across the room to his latest evil invention. "I've invented the Bread-in-ator!" Dr Doofenshmirtz announced. He rubbed his hands together eagerly. Then he pointed to a control panel with a large loaf of bread pictured on the front of it. Perry noticed that on top of the control panel was a giant wire cage. The cage was full of dozens of black and white birds, flapping their wings furiously. Above it all was an

enormous ray gun, aimed right out of the window.
Just what was the doctor up to this time? Agent
P wondered.

"Not only will this machine emit a ray that
will turn Mr President into whole-grain bread,
it will also release a flock of hungry magpies
that will devour the doughy statue!" The evil
doctor laughed maniacally. "Bread go bye-bye!"
he taunted in a sing-song voice.

Perry's mind was already whirring with
ideas. He knew he had to defeat the evil
doctor somehow!

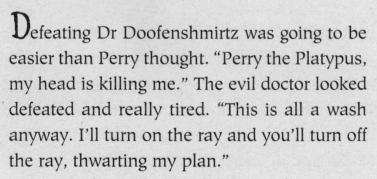

Chapter 6

Defeating Dr Doofenshmirtz was going to be easier than Perry thought. "Perry the Platypus, my head is killing me." The evil doctor looked defeated and really tired. "This is all a wash anyway. I'll turn on the ray and you'll turn off the ray, thwarting my plan."

Agent P kept silent and didn't make a move.

"Let's just get this over with, all right?" the doctor continued. He moved towards the

46

control panel and pulled a large red lever. "Ray on!" he announced.

The ray gun whirred to life and a red-hot glowing beam shot out of the gun and through the window. It was heading right towards the statue! But just then, two workers walked by, carrying a large sheet of glass. Just as the beam was about to strike and destroy the statue, it bounced off the glass and headed in the other direction.

Agent P knew he had to move quickly. He leaped across the room and flipped the ray lever to the OFF position.

"Ray off. Good," Dr Doofenshmirtz said. He was too distracted to notice that the cage door above them had already opened - suddenly there were magpies everywhere! They were on the loose and flying out of the window!

"I'm just going to lie down for a bit," the doctor called to Perry as he shuffled out of the room. "I promise I'll be more evil next time, all right?"

But Agent P's job was far from finished. Someone had to stop the wayward laser beam and flock of magpies from causing any damage! He leaped out of the window, skillfully catching the rope he had used to scale the building earlier and swung into action.

Back at the roller-derby rink, the rematch was over, the fans had gone home and things were returning to normal. Outside the rink, Candace got down to business.

"All right, all right," she told Phineas and Ferb. "We've had our kicks. But mum's still going to flip when she sees this."

She pointed to the giant roller-derby rink behind them. There was no way Phineas could cover up this one!

Just then, the kids heard a car door slam. "Ooh, that's their car!" Candace said excitedly. "You are so busted!" She skated off to greet her parents, leaving Phineas and Ferb alone in the backyard.

Phineas and Ferb looked at each other nervously. Their parents weren't going to be happy about this at all! Phineas had just started brainstorming about what to do when suddenly, a pink laser beam shot through

the sky and hit the side of the roller-derby rink! The rink turned bright pink and started flashing. And then it turned into a gigantic loaf of bread! Phineas and Ferb looked at each other and shrugged. They didn't know what had just happened.

Moments later, Candace came skating out of the house, struggling to stay on her feet.

"Mum! Come on, come on! The boys built a giant roller rink in the backyard!" she called behind her gleefully. Then she stopped dead in her tracks. "Uh . . . a giant loaf of bread?" she said, staring in disbelief at the sight in front of her. She looked accusingly at Phineas.

"I don't know," Phineas told his sister. He

was as shocked as Candace was.

"Mum! Mum! The boys built a giant loaf of bread in the backyard!" Candace yelled, heading back inside.

"What?" Mrs Flynn called from inside the house. "I thought you said it was a roller rink."

But as soon as Candace had gone, things got even crazier! Phineas and Ferb watched as a massive flock of birds suddenly swooped down and started to devour the doughy treat! Little did they know that Dr Doofenshmitz's invention had caused a giant loaf of bread to land in their backyard!

And they also didn't know that Perry the Platypus had chased the birds into the backyard, so they could enjoy the large snack. It was tough being a secret agent, but someone

had to do it!

"Come on!" Candace yelled, as she dragged her mother and father into the backyard. "See?" she said, gesturing wildly.

"Candace, what are you talking about?" her mum asked, giving her daughter a concerned look.

Candace looked at the now-empty backyard. "B-b-b-bread," she stammered. There had been a loaf of bread there just one second ago, she was positive! She stomped her foot angrily. Phineas always got away with everything - it was so unfair!

"Boys, I think that she's finally lost it," Mrs Flynn joked. Mr Fletcher smiled.

"Hey, Dad, how did your speech go?" Phineas asked.

"Well, I have to say it was thimble-y wonderful."

Their dad laughed at his own joke.

Just then, Phineas noticed a remote control with a single red button sitting on the ground between him and Ferb. "Hey, what does this thing do?" he wondered aloud, picking it up. He pressed the red button.

"Wha - " Candace started to say just as the fiery jet engines on her roller skates roared to life. She flew backwards at breakneck speed. "Aaaaahh!" she screamed.

At that very moment, Jeremy strolled into the backyard.

"Hello, you guys. Candace around?" he asked.

Suddenly, Candace rocketed towards Jeremy. They were heading for a major collision! But then, just in time, Jeremy reached out and caught Candace in

his arms.

"Good catch, Jeremy," Ferb said. Phineas nodded in agreement.

Candace gazed up at Jeremy. "He sure is," she said dreamily.

And so ended yet another day of their  summer's holiday. Phineas grinned to himself. It had turned out to be a pretty awesome day, after all!

Part Two

Chapter 1

"And that, ladies and gents, is how I defeated wild tigers in the Amazon," Ferb's Grandpa Reg said as he leaned back in his chair, putting his hands behind his head.

It was another sunny summer morning for Phineas Flynn and Ferb Fletcher - only this one was a little more exciting because Ferb's Grandpa and Grandma Fletcher had arrived from England for a visit! Phineas and Ferb

and the rest of the family were gathered around the kitchen table listening to Grandpa Reg's outrageous stories. He sure had plenty of them!

"Awesome story!" Phineas exclaimed. He loved hearing about the wild adventures Grandpa Reg always seemed to have. If only he could be so lucky!

"Well, I'm sure you're going to hear plenty more fantastical stories during Gram and Gramps' visit," Mr Fletcher said, smiling at his

kids.

"You know, I was thinking we could all head to the mall," Phineas's mum, Mrs Flynn suggested, changing the subject.

"What a splendid idea," Grandma Winnie agreed. "I'd love to treat Candace to some new clothes," she said, winking at Candace.

Candace Flynn, Phineas's and Ferb's sister, clapped her hands excitedly and sprinted to the car. She was not one to miss a shopping opportunity and with her Grandma Winnie treating her, maybe she could finally get the outfit she'd been admiring!

"Hey, Mum, could we just stay at home and hear some more of Grandpa's cool stories?" Phineas asked. He and Ferb preferred to leave the shopping to Candace. Besides, it was the summer holiday and they didn't want to spend it in some stuffy mall!

"Sounds good to me," Mrs Flynn replied.

The rest of the family headed out to the

car while Phineas and Ferb anxiously waited for their grandfather to tell another exciting story.

Grandpa Reg looked at Ferb. "My boy!" he exclaimed. "What's this behind your ear?"

He reached his hand behind Ferb's ear and pulled out a thick, brown leather book.

"It's my scrapbook," he said. He set the huge book down on the table with a loud thump.

Phineas eyed Grandpa Reg suspiciously. "How did you do that?" he asked.

His grandfather smiled. "I may seem like a blarmy ole git now, but when I wasn't so long in the tooth, I had some grand larks and engaged in a fair amount of derring-do," he said in his British accent. He slapped his knee and leaned back in his chair, laughing.

"Translate?" Phineas whispered to Ferb.

"When he was younger, he did a bunch of stuff," Ferb replied matter of factly. Ferb never said much, but he always seemed to know exactly what was going on.

Grandpa Reg opened his scrapbook and flipped to a page filled with black and white photos. "Here I am as a young lad. I made my living working at the family fish and chip shop." He chuckled at the memory. "But I was destined for bigger things."

He turned the page and Phineas and Ferb saw a photo of a young man standing proudly next to an old motorcycle. The man wore a leather helmet and a pair of thick goggles.

"I was known as the Great Flying Fishmonger," Grandpa Reg said proudly, turning another page. "Here's my first jump over my dear mum's tea

society."

Phineas and Ferb stared at the picture of their grandfather soaring high above a group of fancy ladies hosting a tea party. Awesome! Phineas thought.

Grandpa Reg showed them some more pictures of his motorcycle jumps, describing each as he went. "Me jumping a whale. A ton of crumpets. The Queen Mum." Then he stopped.

"But there was one jump that haunts me to this day: McGregor's Gorge of Doom," their grandfather revealed sadly. "People turned out by the thousands to witness me and my trusty motorbike, the Holy Mackerel, make our biggest jump yet." He pointed to a picture of himself smiling and waving, revving his motorcycle engine from a starting line.

Grandpa explained to the boys that just as the brass band started playing, some huge grey

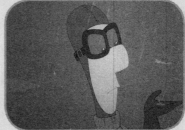

clouds moved in and it began to rain. It became too slippery to perform the jump, so he rescheduled it for a few weeks later. But then he was rained out again!

"And when I made another attempt," Grandpa Reg grumbled as he remembered his third try, "there was nothing but blasted rain again."

Grandpa Reg slammed his scrapbook shut and

grunted as he stood up from the sofa. He walked grumpily across the living room.

Phineas watched him leave. Doing jumps on a motorcycle sounded so cool, he thought. But

not getting to complete the biggest jump of your career would be pretty disappointing - he could understand why Grandpa Reg looked so discouraged.

"Wow, so whatever happened to the Holy Mackerel?" Phineas called after him.

"She's right over there, although I see your mother has turned her into a lamp," Grandpa Reg replied, pointing to a corner of the living room. Phineas took a closer look. The lamp did resemble a motorcycle - one that was shaped suspiciously like a fish.

Suddenly, Phineas had an idea. He was going to surprise Grandpa Reg by rebuilding the gorge in their backyard to give him another chance to jump over it! "Ferb," Phineas said with a twinkle in his eye, "I know what we're going to do today!"

Chapter 2

Meanwhile, Candace was busy running around the mall in a frenzy with her parents and Grandma Winnie. There was nothing she loved more than to shop.

"Oh, Grandma, you're going to love this mall!" she exclaimed. "I'll show you my favourite store and there's this little dress that - " Candace stopped suddenly. She was getting a strange feeling about something. And usually when she got such a feeling, Phineas was involved

somehow. Her brother was always up to something and she constantly had to keep track of him.

Narrowing her eyes, she whipped out her pink mobile phone and speed-dialed her best friend, Stacy Hirano. "Stacy, I have this strange feeling that ground was just broken in my backyard. I need you to get over there and tell me what's going on."

Candace snapped her mobile phone shut. Now that was taken care of and she could get back to what was really important - shopping!

Back at the house, Candace's suspicions were right. There was some major construction

going on! Bulldozers, dump trucks and men with wheelbarrows filled the yard. And right at the centre of it all stood Phineas. He was examining an old photo.

"Judging from this photo of McGregor's Gorge, we're right on track," Phineas reported. He was feeling pretty satisfied with himself for having the idea to re-create Grandpa Reg's motorcycle jump - right in their very own backyard!

Just then, Phineas's friend Isabella Garcia walked up to him. She had a big crush on Phineas, but he never seemed to notice. "Hey, Phineas. Whatcha doin'?" she asked.

"Hey, Isabella," Phineas replied. "We're helping our grandpa fulfill his crushed dreams."

"Where's Ferb?" Isabella asked.

"He's in the garage restoring a mackerel," Phineas told her.

"Cool." Isabella held up a fuzzy yellow stuffed animal. "Well, I brought over this cute little toy for Perry. Where is he?"

Phineas glanced around the backyard, looking for his pet platypus. "Huh. I don't know," Phineas said. Come to think of it, Perry hadn't been around all morning. . . .

Little did Phineas or Ferb know that Perry had a secret life. When he wasn't playing the part of family pet, he was acting as a secret agent, fending off attempts at domination of the tri-state area, launched by the evil Dr Doofenshmirtz.

Right now, Perry - Agent P when he was on duty - was underground in his headquarters,

the high-tech Platypus Cave. Surrounded by computers and gadgets designed to defend against Dr Doofenshmirtz's every attack, Perry was sitting at his desk awaiting orders from his commanding officer.

Suddenly, Carl Karl, Major Monogram's intern, popped up on the jumbo-screen monitor. "Oh. Ha," he laughed nervously. He seemed uncomfortable being on the giant screen. "Hey, Agent P, Monogram's thrown his back out . . ." he started to say.

Perry heard the familiar voice of his superior officer coming from the monitor as well. But he didn't see him anywhere. "I'm on the floor, Agent P," Major Monogram said.

"So I'll be giving you your assignment, okay?" Carl continued. He reached into his coat pocket and pulled

out a note card. He cleared his throat and then began to read:

"Dr Doofenshmirtz has been buying some suspicious items - bags of sand and an extralong shoelace. . . We know he's up to no good. Get out there and see what he's up to!"

Suspicious items surely meant the evil doctor was gearing up for something . . . evil. Perry quickly left the room. He was on the case!

Things above ground were getting interesting as well. Phineas and Ferb were just about to unveil their big backyard surprise to Grandpa Reg. The boys guided him out of the sliding glass door into the yard.

"What's all the kerfuffle, lads?" Grandpa Reg asked, his hands covering his eyes so as not to spoil the surprise.

"You can open your eyes now!" Phineas

told him excitedly.

He slowly opened his eyes. "Blimey!" their grandfather cried. Standing before him was an enormous trench dug right into the backyard and an exact replica of the jump he had never gotten the chance to complete!

Next to the gorge, Ferb was leaning proudly against the ultra-shiny, super-sleek and fully restored Holy Mackerel. Grandpa Reg was stunned. "It's McGregor's Gorge and the Holy Mackerel!" he exclaimed. "Ferb, you've restored my pride and joy!"

Phineas and Grandpa Reg admired the shiny finish Ferb had applied to the fish-shaped bike. But then Grandpa Reg looked down at the ground sadly. "But I can't operate a motorbike in my condition . . ." he began.

Phineas interrupted. "Not a problem. Ferb's tricked out the entire bike - support, padded seating, ergonomic controls." He walked around the motorcycle, pointing out all the features that would help Grandpa Reg make the jump. "And the best part . . ." Phineas paused for dramatic effect. "Sidecars!"

He and Ferb rolled out two gleaming silver sidecars, complete with their own fish tails! They snapped the cars into place on either side of the motorcycle.

"See," Phineas continued, "as much as we

want to help you fulfill your dream, we also really want to jump a gorge," he admitted.

Grandpa Reg looked delighted. "Well, then you'll come with me. The Flying Fishmongers shall jump again!" he proclaimed triumphantly.

Chapter 3

Over at the mall, Candace's sweet shopping spree was turning a bit sour. Somehow her grandmother had steered her into Hail Britannia - just the kind of clothing store perfect for British grandmothers but not for fashionistas like Candace. As Candace tried on yet another outfit, she adjusted her hat and fumed. "Uh, can we get out of here, like, now, before anyone I know happens to see - "

But then Candace heard a male voice call out from the front of the store. "Candace? I almost didn't recognize you."

No, Candace thought. It couldn't be. It just could not be. She would absolutely die of humiliation on the spot if it was Jeremy Johnson, the boy she had a huge crush on. But she would recognize his voice anywhere and it was definitely him!

"Jeremy! I-I, uh . . ." Candace stammered, trying to find a way to look fashionable in her stuffy-looking outfit. She could feel her face turning redder by the second.

But luckily for Candace, Jeremy couldn't stay long. "I have to meet my mum at the food court, but I'll see you later," Jeremy said. He

waved as he continued past the store entrance.

Candace could not believe what had just happened. It was so totally, utterly, completely mortifying. Why do things like this always happen to me? she wondered. Suddenly her mobile phone rang. She quickly answered it.

"Oh, hey, Stacy . . ." Candace listened for a brief moment and then grinned mischievously. She knew her brothers were up to something! "Mum, Stacy just told me the boys built a huge gorge in the backyard!" she shouted.

Her mother rolled her eyes and smiled. Candace was always telling her outrageous things about Phineas and Ferb. "That hat might be a bit too tight," she joked to her husband.

Phineas knew that if they were really going to re-create the scene of Grandpa Reg's big jump they needed to gather a crowd. So he had asked his friend Baljeet to help spread the word about the Holy Mackerel and McGregor's

Gorge of Doom. Baljeet was in the centre of town, wearing a mackerel costume to advertise the event.

"Come see the Flying Fishmongers jump McGregor's Gorge! Tell your friends!" Baljeet shouted.

"Do you know how dumb you look?" Buford Von Stom, the town bully, said, walking over to him.

"I thought this would be a good way to get more attention," Baljeet responded.

Just then a pretty girl passed by and admired Baljeet's costume. "I love your outfit. It's so cute," she cooed.

Buford did a double take. If a mackerel suit could get girls to notice him, he was in! He quickly put on his own fish costume. "Gorge jump!" he

shouted.

Candace, her parents and Grandma Winnie had just left the mall and were heading to their car. As they walked by a TV repair shop, Candace couldn't help but overhear a broadcast on a large TV in the window.

"Come see the Flying Fishmongers jump the gorge, live!" the newsreader urged. Candace glanced at the picture on the TV screen and then pressed her face against the glass in shock. How could this be happening? The broadcast was taking place in her very own backyard! "That's our yard!" she shouted.

"Mum! Mum, come here. I need you to see this!"

"Sponsored by Gorgeous Pore Cream Paste," the newsreader continued. The screen flashed to a picture of skin cream just as Mrs Flynn walked up behind her daughter.

"Oh, honey," she said, looking at the advert and shaking her head. "Your pores aren't that big."

Candace groaned. She had to get back to the house. Finally, Phineas is going to get busted, Candace thought. Sweet!

On the other side of town, Agent P was doing his best to stay incognito. It was of utmost importance for a spy of his calibre to keep his secret identity . . . a secret. In an alley behind Dr Doofenshmirtz's headquarters, the platypus emerged from a skip. He climbed a stack of boxes and then dived behind a plant in the corner. Next he inched his way along a

wall, heading for the back door.

Just as Perry was about to sneak inside, Dr Doofenshmirtz flung the door open and stuck out his head. "Oh, just come in," the doctor said, sounding annoyed.

Agent P shrugged and walked through the

door into Dr Doofenshmirtz's sinister high-tech lab. But all of a sudden, Perry's webbed feet were stuck to the floor and he couldn't move!

"Yes, sticky flypaper, Perry the Platypus!" the doctor exclaimed, laughing evilly. Perry

frowned as he realized he really was trapped. He was in quite the sticky situation!

Dr Doofenshmirtz had Agent P just where he wanted him. He began to explain why he had developed his latest evil invention. "Quick story?" the doctor asked.

Without waiting for Perry's answer, he continued, "Back in Drusselstein, in the days of my youth, there was a bully named Boris who always wore big, black boots. They called him 'Big, Black Boots Boris the Bully.'" Dr Doofenshmirtz shuddered at the memory and kept talking.

"He was always kicking sand in my face.

When I was in the sandbox: sand. My first date: sand. Balancing my checkbook: sand! The beach . . ." Dr Doofenshmirtz paused and thought for a moment. "Oddly enough, nothing. But I couldn't relax because I kept waiting for it."

Dr Doofenshmirtz went on. "Now he will be the one doing the waiting," he said in an evil voice. The doctor held up a remote control. With his finger poised above a large red button, he bellowed, "Behold! The Now-Who's-Blinded-by-Sand-inator!" Then he considered what he had just said. "Or maybe the Who's-Crying-Now-inator!"

Dr Doofenshmirtz pushed a button and Perry watched as the walls of the room collapsed around them to reveal a giant boot. Rising out of the boot was a huge, rotating propeller like device with a giant bucket

dangling from its end.

"It's a giant sand-kicking machine," Dr Doofenshmirtz explained. He and Perry were already in the cockpit!

Agent P, still stuck on the flypaper, balled his fists. The evil doctor would not get away with this!

"You see, Perry the Platypus," the doctor said as he revved the engine, "Boris has moved to the tri-state area, so I am going to cover his entire house in sand! Ah-ha-ha!"

Suddenly, the doctor's latest invention roared to life and whisked Perry and Dr Doofenshmirtz up into the sky! Perry was going to have to come up with a way to get out of this latest mishap - and fast!

Chapter 4

In their backyard, Phineas, Ferb and Grandpa Reg stood on top of an enormous launch ramp. A large crowd had gathered to watch the event. *Advertising really pays off!* Phineas thought. He reached for a microphone. "And now, what you've all come to see . . . The Flying Fishmongers!" Phineas announced. The crowd cheered wildly.

"And here to play the Fishmongers' anthem

are Isabella and the Fireside Girls!" The Fireside Girls were members of Isabella's scout troop.

"Hit it!" Phineas shouted.

From a nearby gazebo, the girls began to play the slow, gloomy song that Grandpa Reg remembered so well from his earlier gorge-jumping attempts. But as they sang the lyrics, the sky above them darkened and there was a great clap of thunder. CRACK! Then it started

to rain, drenching everyone in the crowd.

Grandpa Reg shook his head, disappointed. After all these years, the rain had ruined his plans yet again. "Well, my boy, looks like I'll never get to fulfill my dream," he told Ferb.

Phineas was very confused. There hadn't been a cloud in the sky a moment ago! How could this be?

"Hey, guys," he called to Isabella and the Fireside Girls. "You can stop playing." The girls put down their instruments. Then, the rain stopped suddenly, the clouds broke and the sun came out.

Phineas looked up at the sky. "Wait a second . . ." he began. He had an idea! "Start again!" he told Isabella.

The band struck up the same dull tune once

more. And sure enough, the clouds moved in and it started to rain again.

"Stop!" Phineas commanded. "Start!" With each pause in the dull music, the sky cleared up. And with each new start, the rain rolled in. It was as if the Fishmonger anthem was controlling the weather!

"Grandpa, the song is so dreary it's causing it to rain!" Phineas exclaimed. "What if we pep it up a bit?" he suggested.

"Pep away, my boy," Grandpa Reg said heartily.

"Hey, Isabella, crank it up a notch!" Phineas yelled.

"Okey dokey! Ready, girls?" Isabella said. Then she and the Fireside Girls began to play a funky, upbeat song that got the whole crowd moving. Phineas waited to see if his theory was correct and sure enough, it was! The

skies cleared up and the sun shone brightly. Now Grandpa's gorge jump could continue as planned!

On top of the platform, Grandpa Reg sat on the Holy Mackerel and Phineas and Ferb jumped into their sidecars. Their grandfather revved the motorcycle engine and stepped on the accelerator. They zoomed down the ramp and sailed out over the gorge, aiming right for the landing point on the other side.

Phineas couldn't believe it - they were going to make the jump! But then, they all realized that they weren't going to clear the

gorge after all! Before they knew it, Grandpa Reg, Phineas and Ferb found themselves plummeting through the air, falling faster and faster toward the bottom of the gorge!

"Maybe we should have let it rain," Grandpa Reg yelled as they dived down toward the ground.

"Don't worry!" Phineas called out. "We've got a backup plan. Ferb?"

Ferb reached for a lever in his sidecar's cockpit and yanked it backwards. A pair of razor-thin wings shot out from both sides. The motorcycle righted its course and glided

swiftly up and out of the gorge! But then, in the very next instant, one of the Mackerel's wings clipped a branch and snapped in half.

"That can't be good," Phineas said.

The next thing they knew, Phineas, Ferb and Grandpa Reg were careening across the sky again. They'd completely lost control of the Holy Mackerel! What were they going to do now?

Chapter 5

Candace was staring anxiously out of the backseat window of the family car as they drove home from their shopping trip. It seemed that the ride was taking forever and all Candace wanted was to get home and finally get Phineas in trouble!

All of a sudden, she noticed a strange object flying through the air. Could that be . . . ? Candace shook her head in disbelief. There was

no way Grandpa Reg, Phineas and Ferb could have gotten their hands on a flying motorcycle! Or could they have? "Dad, can we speed this pony ride up a little?" she asked anxiously.

"Honey, I'll have you ladies home in two shakes of a lamb's tail," her father replied. Then he suddenly slammed on the brakes and patiently waited for a turtle to cross the street. Candace sighed. At this rate, they were never going to get there!

Back inside the Holy Mackerel, Phineas and Ferb were struggling to regain control of their

runaway motorcycle. They spun out of the sky and landed with a thud on top of a train that was barrelling along a bridge over a river. Just before the train entered a tunnel, the Holy Mackerel slid off - and was headed for the water below!

Thinking quickly, Ferb broke off the

remaining wing and threw it under the vehicle like a surfboard. The Holy Mackerel surfed right onto the riverbank . . . and kept going! It

slid across the grass, into a neighbour's yard and onto an inflatable castle.

Suddenly, the castle catapulted the Holy Mackerel back up into the sky and then the motorcycle landed right smack where it had started - at the top of the jump ramp in Phineas and Ferb's backyard!

With all the extra momentum, the Holy Mackerel began to coast down the ramp, picking up even more speed. The motorcycle launched itself out over the gorge and sailed through the air. Everything seemed to be happening in slow motion. The faces in the crowd were staring up at the motorcycle in shock.

Then, with a thud, the Holy Mackerel made a miraculous landing on the other side of the gorge! The crowd erupted in cheers.

Wow, what a ride! Phineas thought, both relieved and exhilarated. McGregor's Gorge had proved no match for the new Holy

Mackerel!

"Good show, my boys! Good show!" Grandpa Reg cheered and congratulated Phineas and Ferb. They had helped him achieve his lifelong dream!

Meanwhile, evil Dr Doofenshmirtz's sand-kicking contraption was flying across the sky toward Boris the Bully's house, with Perry still aboard.

"Ha-ha, the home of my former nemesis!" The evil doctor cackled. "Time to kick a little

sand, eh, Perry the Platypus?"

Perry fixed his eyes on his nemesis and leaped out of his shoes, leaving them still stuck to the flypaper. Perry had been secretly wearing shoes the whole time - ones that looked exactly like his very own feet! He stood in his white and blue striped tube socks, glaring at Dr Doofenshmirtz.

"Tube socks?" The villain looked shocked, but then got back to business. "Well, it's too late now. . . ." The doctor pushed the button on his remote control. Under them, the giant boot wound up, preparing to kick a huge bucketful of sand right over Boris's house.

Finally! Dr Doofensmirtz thought gleefully. After all of these years, I will get my revenge against terrible Boris the Bully!

But Perry had an idea. He was not going to let the evil doctor get away with this. Just as the boot was aiming for the bucket, the platypus raced across the cockpit and leaped

onto Dr Doofenshmirtz's back.

"What are you doing?" the evil doctor cried.

This had not been part of his plan!

Chapter 6

Back at Phineas and Ferb's house, the boys and Grandpa Reg were relaxing after accomplishing their awesome feat.

"Thank you, lads, for helpin' this old codger fulfill his dreams," Grandpa Reg said happily.

Just then, Candace came storming across the yard.

"You guys are sooo busted," she announced, taking in the scene of the giant gorge behind

them. "Look at this. It's even better than I thought. There's no way you're going to get out of this one!" She ran gleefully back towards the house. "Oh, Mum! Muuuuuum!"

But what Candace didn't know was that Dr Doofenshmirtz's invention was hovering dangerously close to Phineas and Ferb's backyard. The doctor was struggling to maintain control of his contraption as he wrestled with Perry, who was still attached to his back. "Cut it out, Perry the Platypus!" he yelled.

Suddenly, the doctor lost his grip on his remote control and it tumbled to the ground below. "Ha! No stopping it now!" Dr Doofenshmirtz proclaimed, watching the

controller get smaller and smaller as it fell.

And he was right. His boot and sand bucket contraption was already in motion. The big mechanical boot kicked the metal bucket, sending tons of sand into the air. It looked like Boris the Bully was in for a sandstorm.

But just then, an unexpected gust of wind swirled through the air. It picked up the falling sand and sent it flying right back in Dr Doofenshmirtz's direction! Perry ducked as the sand blasted toward them and covered the evil doctor from head to toe.

All of a sudden, the metal bucket swung backwards and knocked right into the giant boot. The boot broke off and plummeted towards the ground below - heading right for Phineas and Ferb's backyard! And it was aimed directly for a row of dump trucks full of dirt that Phineas and Ferb had dug out to form McGregor's Gorge!

The boot slammed down onto the trucks,

causing them to tip over and send the dirt flying into the air - and right back into the gorge it had come out of. It hardly looked like a hole had been dug at all anymore!

Perry calmly watched the chaos below. Then he quietly unfolded a hang glider, jumped into the air and flew away from the sand kicking machine. A moment later, Dr Doofenshmirtz spiraled away in his destroyed contraption. "Curse you, Perry the Platypus!" he shouted.

At the Fletcher-Flynn house, Grandpa Reg still couldn't get over all that had happened.

"I must tell you, I love the new anthem," he remarked. Phineas had also thought the peppy new tune was a huge improvement over the dreary original.

At that moment, Perry the Platypus waddled into the yard. "Hey, Perry," Phineas said.

"But I do miss the old one," Grandpa Reg continued, thinking about the familiar song that brought back such memories. "Couldn't I hear it one last time?"

"You got it, Grandpa! One last time, girls!" Phineas exclaimed.

Isabella and the Fireside Girls cranked out the old song one more time. And sure enough, in rolled the clouds. Then it started to rain, causing new grass to sprout in the dirt that had refilled the gorge. Phineas and Ferb looked on in amazement. That is pretty cool! Phineas thought.

"These two have really done it this time, Mum," Candace was telling her mother as the song ended. "Look what they did to the backyard." She dragged her mum to the spot where the gorge had been.

"Wow!" her mum exclaimed. "You guys made the lawn look great! Oh, it's all weeded

and watered. Well done!"

Candace's mouth dropped open in shock. There had been a giant hole there a moment ago! It looked as if Phineas was going to get away with another one of his schemes. How did he do it?

"So what else did you do today?" Mrs Flynn asked, while leading the boys and Grandpa Reg inside.

"Well, these two roister-doisters wheeled out me old iron, built a crackin' match for McGregor's Gorge and helped this daft ole git have one last knees-up," Grandpa Reg told her happily.

Phineas gave Ferb a baffled look. What was their grandfather talking about?

"I have absolutely no idea," Ferb replied, knowing exactly what Phineas was thinking.

Phineas smiled. It had been a spectacular day. Grandpa Reg had finally accomplished his lifelong dream and he and Ferb had managed to jump a gorge - in sidecars, no less! Just as Phineas had suspected, re-creating one of Grandpa Reg's outrageous stories was way better than simply listening to one. Hmm, I wonder what we can re-create next! Phineas thought.

Don't miss the fun in the next
Phineas & Ferb book...

Freeze Frame

Adapted by Ellie O'Ryan
Based on the series created by Dan Povenmire & Jeff "Swampy" Marsh

Phineas Flynn and Ferb Fletcher grinned at each other across the dining room table as they ate dinner with their family. It had been a perfect summer's day; warm sun, gentle breezes and an exciting trip to the moon. The brothers were pretty pleased with themselves.

But across the table, their older sister, Candace Flynn, was not pleased at all. She put down her fork and pouted. "But Mum, it's true!" she complained. "The boys built a lift to the moon in the backyard today!"

Mrs Flynn shook her head. "Last time I checked, the yard was noticeably 'moon lift' free," their mum said patiently.

"But - " Candace sputtered.

Phineas felt bad. He and Ferb thought Candace was a great big sister and they didn't mean to drive her crazy. They didn't even mind that Candace spent most of her time trying to get them in trouble. So Phineas decided to speak up in her defense.

"It's true," he said, nodding his head. "We were up there. Ferb did the whole 'one giant step' thing. Check out this moon stuff we

brought back." He held out a handful of moon rocks, while Ferb waved an American flag - the one that Neil Armstrong had planted forty years earlier!

Candace crossed her arms and smirked.

But their mum just smiled at Phineas and Ferb.

"Oh, you boys are just so adorable," their dad said proudly.

"Ugh! You don't really believe it!" Candace exclaimed. "I'm so over this!"

"Oh, Candace," her mum said with a sigh. "Revel in your brothers' imaginations. It makes life so much more fun!" She stood up and started to clear the table.

Phineas stretched and yawned. "Pushing the boundaries of time and space sure makes a guy tired," he said.

"See?" Mrs Flynn asked. "How fun is that?"

But Candace just shook her head. She didn't think there was anything fun about living with Phineas and Ferb. In fact, ever since her mum had married Ferb's dad and Ferb had officially become her stepbrother, Candace had been constantly annoyed by the pair. They did one crazy thing after another - and they never got in trouble for any of it!

But Phineas and Ferb had been thrilled when Phineas' mum married Ferb's dad. They felt more like real brothers than stepbrothers - and, even better, they were best friends too!

Rubbing their eyes and yawning, Phineas and Ferb got up from the table and walked over to the staircase. After their exciting adventures that day, they were ready for bed.

"'Night, boys," Mr Fletcher said in his very proper English accent.

"'Night, mopey," Mrs Flynn teased Candace.

Candace slumped off toward the stairs without even responding to her mum. No matter what shenanigans Phineas and Ferb tried, no one ever believed Candace. Her parents always thought she was the crazy one!

"'See? How fun is that?'" she said grumpily, repeating her mum. "If only they'd believe me!" Candace sighed. She knew that without proof - without cold, hard, undeniable proof - Phineas and Ferb would continue to get away with their usual stunts.